The Christmas Drum

The Christmas Drum

Maureen Brett Hooper
illustrated by Diane Paterson

Boyds Mills Press

To Jennifer, our Christmas Angel
—M.B.H.

For my husband, John
—D.P.

This story is based on field research done by Dr. Ann Schuursma,
Fulbright Research Scholar. Special thanks to her for the time
and interest she gave this project and for permission to use her
translation of the carol in this story.

Text copyright © 1994 by Maureen Brett Hooper
Illustrations copyright © 1994 by Diane Paterson
All rights reserved
Published by Caroline House
Boyds Mills Press, Inc.
A Highlights Company
815 Church Street
Honesdale, Pennsylvania 18431
Printed in Mexico

Publisher Cataloging-in-Publication Data
Hooper, Maureen Brett.
The Christmas drum / [by] Maureen Brett Hooper ;
illustrated by Diane Paterson.—1st ed.
[32]p. : col. ill. ; cm.
Summary : Filling in for his father, a young boy plays
the drum in the traditional *colindat* on Christmas Eve.
ISBN 1-56397-105-4
1. Christmas stories, Romanian—Juvenile literature.
[1. Christmas stories, Romanian.] I. Paterson, Diane, ill. II. Title.
[E]—dc20   1994   CIP
Library of Congress Catalog Card Number 93-73308

First edition, 1994
The text of this book is set in 14-point Palatino.
The illustrations are done in watercolors.
Distributed by St. Martin's Press

10 9 8 7 6 5 4 3 2 1

About the Christmas Drum

Each year on Christmas Eve, in countries all over the world, people celebrate the coming of Christmas with the joyous custom of caroling. In Romania this custom is called the *colindat*. In some of the villages the custom is called the *colindat cu duba,* or *colindat* with drum, because a few of the carolers not only sing but play a drum called the *duba.* This tiny drum is played just once a year on the night of the *colindat.* It brings a noisy excitement to these celebrations.

For weeks before Christmas arrives, the musicians go to the home of the villager with the largest house, where they rehearse for the *colindat.* The music they sing and play is very old and has never been written down. The older men must teach the music to the younger men—word by word, note by note, rhythm by rhythm.

On Christmas Eve, the men of the *colindat* walk from house to house, with the *duba* players leading the way. At each home they go inside to sing their carols, dance with the girls, and wish the family good health and happiness in the year to come. Everywhere they go they are welcomed and given gifts.

When all the houses have been visited, they return to the home of the villager with the largest house. Once there, they divide their gifts, sing one last carol, and say good night.

And the *colindat* is over for another year.

D eep in a river valley, in a country called Romania, there was a little village. In that village there lived a boy named Peter. One morning when it was hardly light, Peter opened his eyes and looked down at the Christmas drum nestled at the foot of his bed. "Dear *duba*," he whispered to the tiny drum. "Tonight is Christmas Eve!"

As long as Peter could remember, Papa had played the drum for the *colindat* on Christmas Eve. Each year, when it was time, he would take down the drum and wave good-bye to the family. And soon Peter would hear the *duba* echoing through the village, telling everyone the carolers were on their way.

But this year Papa would not be there to lead the *colindat*. This year Peter was supposed to play the *duba*. It seemed a very difficult thing, and he was not at all sure that he could do it.

Peter sat up. "Oh, dear *duba*," he said. "How terrible it will be if I'm not good enough to take Papa's place tonight."

Peter left his tiny alcove bed. Already the others in his family were awake, and the house was filled with the sounds and smells of Christmas Eve.

Grandfather, humming a merry carol, warmed himself by the stove. "For eighty-and-one years I've sung this song," he said.

Peter's sister, Anna, tapping her foot in time to Grandfather's tune, embroidered the last flower on her new dress—a dress like the one Mama wore. "Tonight I know someone will ask me to dance," she said.

Mama, smiling to herself, was making sausages and sweet Christmas bread to give to the carolers that night. "Mine will be the best in the village," she said.

Peter stood firmly in the middle of the room. He held the *duba* for them to see. "Do you really think I can take Papa's place tonight?" he asked.

Grandfather smiled at him. Anna and Mama stopped what they were doing.

"Of course," Mama said reassuringly.

Still, Peter wished Papa would come home.

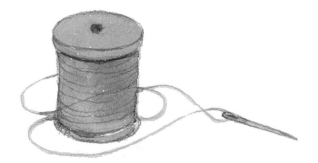

Later, Peter went to the valley road when the bus from the city was due. He hoped it would bring Papa at last. But when all the other passengers climbed down, Papa was still not there.

Weeks ago he had gone to the city. He had been sent there to work in the big factory. "If I don't get back in time," he said to Peter, "you must play my *duba* on Christmas Eve."

And Peter had promised.

Then one night the *colindat* rehearsals began. Peter remembered his promise and hurried to Great-papa Ion's house.

He held the Christmas drum high for all the men to see. "I've come to play Papa's *duba*," he shouted. "I've come to sing the carols."

The shepherd piper stopped piping; the accordion player stopped squeezing; the singers stopped singing. They frowned at Peter and shook their heads as if they knew he could never play the Christmas drum or sing the carols.

Peter cringed beneath their looks, but he did not move.

Then little-pig Purcica said, "Well, you are small, but I suppose you won't eat too much."

And girl-crazy Fetelar said, "Well, you are young, but I suppose you won't dance with the girls."

And tired-old Borbirau said, "Well, you are likely to fall asleep, but I suppose that's not such a terrible thing to do."

They voted to let Great-papa Ion decide.

The old man shook his finger in Peter's face. "You must be on time and never go to sleep. For if you do, you must ride through the village on a mule with a bell round its neck—just as our friend here did last year." He pointed to a sheepish Borbirau.

And though the thought of the mule ride made Peter shake all over, he stayed.

He went every night to Great-papa Ion's house. He was always on time. Never once did he fall asleep.

Night after night he tried to play the *duba*. Night after night he tried to sing the carols. But the men only frowned and shook their heads.

With each night poor Peter grew more worried. *Maybe I'm too young*, he thought. *Maybe I'm too small.*

Still, when the sun set and Christmas Eve arrived at last, Peter put on his Sunday clothes, decorated the *duba* with a wreath of pine, and waited for the *colindat* to begin.

As the hour grew close Peter hugged the tiny drum. And when the clock struck nine, he said a special prayer for Papa's help, waved good-bye to his family, and ran all the way to Great-papa Ion's house.

The men of the *colindat* were already there, dressed in their very best. Down the road the houses glowed, and children peeked from every window.

Peter stepped to the middle of the road. A quiet spread over the village. It was time to begin.

But when he went to strike the drum, his hand turned to stone. "Dear *duba*," he whispered. "I *am* too young. I *am* too small. I *can't* take Papa's place!"

Then Peter was sure he heard the drum reply, "You can! You can!"

So Peter started down the road. And soon he was playing as he had never played before.

The shepherd piper heard him and joined in. His melodies twinkled like stars against the cold night air. The accordion player, not to be outdone, pushed and pulled in a most spectacular manner.

Little-pig Purcica fell into place. Over his shoulder he threw the long bag that would hold their gifts of sausages and sweet Christmas bread. Girl-crazy Fetelar followed, tapping his toes wildly to the beat. And some distance back, tired-old Borbirau came. He puffed and snorted as he walked.

Peter and the men stopped at each house along the road. In storms of laughter they rushed inside. They sang until the rafters shivered. They danced until the walls shook. Purcica's bag filled with sausages and sweet Christmas bread.

Through it all Peter played the drum. And the people marveled. "There has never been such a *duba* player," they said.

It was midnight when Peter led the way to his own house. His feet were stiff with cold, and his fingers ached.

He saw Mama standing in the doorway and his heart pounded. Anna was there in her dress just like the one Mama wore. And Grandfather stood behind them.

"Come in, come in," they called out.

Peter played the *duba* for his family as the men of the *colindat* sang their carols.

Purcica held out his bag for Mama's sausages and sweet Christmas bread. "It's the best in all the village," he said.

Fetelar bowed and asked Anna to dance. She giggled as he twirled her about.

And Borbirau, poor Borbirau, propped his chin upon his hands and worked to stay awake.

Then it was time for Peter's favorite carol. The men of the *colindat* nudged him forward to sing alone. His voice soared:

There, on a part of the earth,
There up high, and higher up,
There up high toward the sunrise
In the white courtyard of Christmas,
At the time when the Lord was born,
Torches burned in pear trees.
In the white courtyard of Christmas,
While he was born in a stable,
Flowers grew on branches,
Dew fell upon the flowers,
And the scent of the dew
Spread over the earth.

When Peter finished singing, Mama wiped a tear from her eye. Grandfather cleared his throat and blew his nose. And Anna sighed.

Suddenly a loud voice boomed from the doorway, "Ah, my little *duba* player."

Peter whirled around. "Papa! You've come," he cried out as he ran to Papa's arms.

Papa laughed and smiled as he swung Peter into the air.

"Oh, Papa, I took your place for the *colindat*."

"So I see," Papa said.

"I sang a carol all alone."

"I heard you singing as I came up the road."

"Oh, Papa, I stayed awake. Now I won't have to ride the mule with a bell round its neck. And oh, Papa, all night long people cheered for me as I played your *duba*."

Papa nodded. He seemed pleased. "Peter," he said, "now it is your *duba*."

Peter's eyes grew heavy.

Gently, Papa carried him to his tiny alcove bed. "Sleep well, my little *duba* player," he said as he pulled the covers to Peter's chin and tucked the *duba* by his side.

"Good night, my dear *duba*," Peter said softly to his Christmas drum.

"Good night, good night," the drum whispered back.

And soon Peter was asleep, dreaming of drums and sausages and sweet Christmas bread.